W9-DFV-842

ONE GOAL

N.J. CORBO

One Goal
Heads or Tails

Copyright © 2015

Published by Scobre Educational

Written by N.J. Corbo

Series created by Josh Anderson

All rights reserved.

Printed in the United States of America.

No part of this book may be reproduced in any manner whatsoever without written permission, except in the case of brief quotations embodied in critical articles and reviews.

Scobre Educational
2255 Calle Clara
La Jolla, CA 92037

Scobre Operations & Administration
42982 Osgood Road
Fremont, CA 94539

www.scobre.com
info@scobre.com

Scobre Educational publications may be purchased for educational, business, or sales promotional use.

Cover and layout design by Jana Ramsay
Copyedited by Renae Reed

ISBN: 978-1-62920-257-0 (Soft Cover)
ISBN: 978-1-62920-256-3 (Library Bound)
ISBN: 978-1-62920-255-6 (eBook)

ONE GOAL

N.J. CORBO

A **Heads or Tails** *Adventure in High School Soccer*

Huntington City
Township Public Library
255 West Park Drive
Huntington, IN 46750

Scobre Educational

HOW TO READ THIS BOOK

You should start a **Heads or Tails** book like any other, on page 1. At the bottom of each page, you'll see a direction to move on to the next page, *or* you'll be presented with a choice: *Heads or Tails?*

Heads   Tails

Flip a coin (or just pick randomly), and turn to either the "heads" page or the "tails" page to continue the story. Or, you can read more about each option, and choose the path that sounds the best to you.

You can read this book over and over and never take the same path twice. Enjoy your journey into the glory and agony of high school soccer!

Darrington High School Eagles – Key Players

Chuck Grady, Goal Keeper, Senior
Chuck is a big guy and an aggressive player who can punt the ball far down the field with great precision. It's not uncommon to see Chuck come out to the edge of the penalty box or beyond to play like a sort of second sweeper. Not much gets by him.

Deacon Morris, Midfielder, Junior
Tough as a defensive midfielder, Deacon has a lot of determination, but he also has uncommonly strong technical abilities for his position. Plus, he's good in the air, winning and challenging for headers.

Darby Morris, Forward, Senior
The top scorer on the team. Darby is big and tall, often playing center forward. He knows how to put the ball in the back of the net, and he loves doing it. He's often favored by other teammates to receive the ball.

Evan Johnson, Forward, Junior
Evan is a solid player, but sometimes struggles with controlling the ball. He's got great instincts though, and can be absolutely ruthless.

Jason Burke, Forward, Junior
Small and speedy, Jason likes to cause problems for defenders. He often drops deeper than the other strikers, which makes him available to jump on chances in the penalty box.

Kevin Faklaw, Midfielder, Freshman
(Plays for Weston Soccer Club, too.)
That's YOU! Happiest when the ball is in your possession, you understand how to manage space, because you have the ability to anticipate – especially when on the attack. You're quick, you've got a great shot, and you can dribble past defenders with ease. Plus, you've got a precision flip throw. You always hit your mark.

For a lot of kids, summer is a time to swim, ride bikes, or just hang out with friends. It's a break from schedules and routines – a time to just play without a plan. Even though this was your last summer before high school, you're not like most kids, and you definitely *do* have a plan. So, you spent your summer practicing.

You are Kevin Faklaw, and you live to play soccer. You're a midfielder and, when you're on the attack, watch out. It's as though the ball sticks to you, and you weave through opponents like water around rocks, always finding the path of least resistance. When you're on the field, everything around you slows down and, with a scary level of accuracy, you're able to anticipate what other players will do next. This allows you to deliver goal-scoring passes to strikers, but you love the glory of scoring, and sometimes you just don't want to let it go. As for your plan, it's going to the Olympics someday and bringing home a gold medal. Sometimes, it's all you think about.

You're a decisive and precise player too. Take your flip throw – you can hit your mark as though he was magnetized and the ball was a magnet. Your best friend, Autumn, calls it your super power. Your older sister, Sam, teases you because you always have a soccer ball with you. She's a good player too, but she dropped out of soccer club this fall. She's been spending a lot of time with her boyfriend, Joey. He's a hockey player and, every time he leaves the ice, he takes off his helmet, flips his hair back, and announces himself by saying, "Jo-aaay!" It's hilarious. You like him because he's funny, but you

Go on to the next page.

can't imagine giving up soccer club for anything or anybody.

As older sisters go, Sam is pretty cool, but today she's in the mood to mess with you. Standing next to your parents' car, jingling the keys, she gets a mischievous look on her face.

"I still need a few more hours of supervised driving before I can get my license, so Dad's letting me drive to get dinner," she says, bending to pick up the garden hose. "So, let's go," Sam demands.

"Why do I have to go with . . . " but before you can get all the words out, a stream of water hits your face.

"I dunno, ask Dad," she says, continuing to spray you.

"Hey, quit it," you say, even though the cool water feels good. You've been juggling your soccer ball for an hour and it's at least a million degrees. "Autumn's coming over," you continue to protest, "I don't want to leave."

"Oh, your *girlfriend* is coming over," she taunts, overemphasizing the word 'girl.'

"Seriously, Sam?" You can't believe she still makes fun of you about Autumn.

"*Seriously, Sam?*" she mimics with mock annoyance, as she slides into the driver's seat and turns on the radio. It's so loud that it would be pointless to respond, so you go back to juggling and ignore her.

Besides, it's only the oldest and lamest joke ever. You've known Autumn since the two of you started playing soccer in the Midget Division of the Weston Soccer Club – practically your whole life. You

Go on to the next page.

play on the boys' team and she's on the girls' team now, but you're still really close. Your parents even became friends. Autumn is your best friend, not your girlfriend. Well, technically, she and Bowie are both your best friends.

The three of you became best friends in third grade. You were grouped together for a science project and it ended up being the most fun you had all year. Bowie is super smart – like mad scientist smart – and he had read about using a pickle to conduct and receive electricity. You and Autumn helped build the contraption, but Bowie ran all the wires and set up the electrical parts. When the electric current ran into the pickle, it glowed red – it was so cool. Bowie definitely could have skipped a few grades, but you're happy his parents wanted him to have a normal school experience.

Ever since that project, you've been an inseparable trio. This summer, you spent most of your weekends at Bowie's. You and Autumn practiced soccer moves, while Bowie worked on his inventions, then the three of you would test the gadgets together. Even though Bowie has never shared your love of soccer, he appreciates your dedication to it. He even built a mechanical foot that kicks balls to you. It was his way of joining the game.

Hooonk!

Your sister hits the horn to make you lose your concentration. You think about grabbing the garden hose, but see Autumn running over. Just then, Sam starts the car.

Go on to the next page.

"Ladies and gentlemen, it's the amazing Autumn Jeffers," your dad announces, as he walks onto the porch. He's such a dork sometimes.

"Hey, Mr. Faklaw," Autumn waves, crossing the driveway behind the car.

That's when Sam puts the car in reverse. It lunges back, you yell for her to stop, but it's too late – she hits Autumn.

You dad runs to the back of the car and tells you to get your mom. Sam jumps out screaming and crying. Autumn isn't moving. You're completely freaked out, but you do as you're told; you run to get your mom.

"MOM!" you yell, as you smash through the screen door and practically trip over your dog, Lucy.

"Hey, watch it with the door," she starts to scold you, but sees the look on your face. "Kevin, what is it?"

"Sam hit Autumn with the car. She's not moving."

Luckily, when you get back, she's conscious. She just bumped her head when she fell. Sam's a mess though, pacing and babbling. Lucy runs past you and licks Autumn's face, which makes her giggle. She seems alright. Still, your mom insists on calling Autumn's parents and going to the hospital.

Sitting next to Autumn in the car, you feel anxious, similar to the way you feel before a big game, but different. Maybe you're just worried about her. Instinctually, you grab Autumn's hand and squeeze it tightly. She squeezes back, and something strange happens. Your

Go on to the next page.

skin tingles. Embarrassed, you let go of her quickly and look out the window.

The doctor says Autumn will be okay, but her parents have to monitor her. After the hospital, everyone comes back to your house for Chinese food. They're all laughing and joking, but you and Sam just sit there with your untouched food. Sam is still shaken up, and you can't stop thinking about how Autumn made your skin tingle. Maybe you actually do like her more than a friend. But that would be crazy. But if you do, how should you act?

"I'm sorry my sister drove over you," you try to joke.

"I did not drive over her!" Sam blurts out. "I didn't even see her. I mean, who runs behind a moving car anyway?"

"It's okay, Sam," your mom says peacefully, shaking her head at you. "We all know it was an accident and, sweetie, Autumn is okay," she says, gently rubbing Sam's back. Your mom has a way of making people feel better.

"Oh my gosh," Autumn gasps, grabbing your arm.

"What?" you practically jump out of your seat.

"I almost forgot why I was running over in the first place," she says. "My dad talked to Coach Oliver from the high school. He's going to offer you a spot on the varsity team."

"Is that true?" your dad asks Mr. Jeffers.

"Sure is," he says. "Oliver's an old buddy of mine. He knows it'll be tough to choose between Weston and the varsity team, but he hopes

Go on to the next page.

Kevin will consider it. I think it's a great opportunity, personally."

For the next 20 minutes, your dad and Mr. Jeffers discuss the pros and cons of high school soccer versus club soccer. They talk about how the high school team is All-State and playing against upperclassmen would challenge you, but staying with the club means you'll continue working with an A-list coach and playing with other elite players. They talk about the importance of friendships and bonds made through high school sports, but then there's the fact that some of your best and oldest friends are at Weston. If it wasn't for the U.S. Soccer Development Academy's 10-month season, you could do both.

After dinner, you call Bowie. You need an outside opinion about this soccer decision, and you're also tempted to tell him that you might really like Autumn, but you don't. He's not much help on the soccer front, unfortunately; he just says it seems like everything is changing. You agree. You've got some big decisions ahead of you.

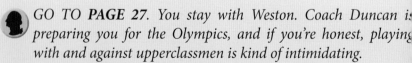

GO TO **PAGE 27**. *You stay with Weston. Coach Duncan is preparing you for the Olympics, and if you're honest, playing with and against upperclassmen is kind of intimidating.*

GO TO **PAGE 38**. *You go with varsity. It wouldn't hurt to know some older guys as a freshman, and this could be another route to the Olympics.*

You really wanted to show off your flip throw for the scout, but it's too risky. You might injure your wrist worse. It's okay though; your offensive abilities will get his attention.

You grab the ball, take a few steps back, and position your hands, thumbs together. Your wrist feels sore but solid. Scanning the field, you see that Darby is open. Your aim is as good as always, but without the extra momentum of the flip, the ball falls short, giving Redmond's defensive midfielder just enough time to snag it.

He kicks it long and everyone goes after it. Now you're on the defense. Their attacking midfielder is out in front. He goes one-on-one with your keeper. He shoots and Chuck reaches to grab it, but misses. Luckily, his shot is just wide of the mark.

Chuck boots it out. Deacon heads it and you connect. Redmond players gather in front of you, but you weave through. It's tight. You want to make the shot – show that scout what you can do. No, there's no space for you. You kick it behind you to the left, passing to Darby. He has a clear shot and, even though their goalie tries to deflect it, the ball goes into the corner. One goal for Darrington.

You get to show off your dribbling skills a couple more times, but Darrington and Redmond are really well matched. After that first goal, their defense turns up the heat. Still, when that final whistle comes, it's Darrington's win.

Winning your first varsity game is great, but you don't know if the scout noticed you. He's sitting on the bleachers, writing. You

Go on to the next page.

decide to talk to him.

"Hey there, number 7," he says, "I heard about your dribbling skills from Coach Duncan. Impressive. Was hoping to see your handspring toss too." For a moment you regret your decision to spare your wrist, but he says that you made a good call to protect it. He thinks you showed great decision making on the field too, because you didn't overplay the ball. You showed that you know when and how to work with your teammates, like the backward pass. He gives you his card and tells you to call.

You don't know how the day could get better. Then Deacon and Darby invite you to meet back at the bleachers after hitting the locker room. A bunch of the guys are going to celebrate. It should be a no-brainer, because you definitely want to show that you can hang, but it's Bowie's birthday, and Sam is waiting to drive you there.

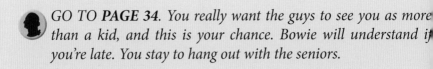 GO TO **PAGE 34**. *You really want the guys to see you as more than a kid, and this is your chance. Bowie will understand if you're late. You stay to hang out with the seniors.*

GO TO **PAGE 14**. *You're psyched, but it's Bowie's birthday and you don't want to blow off your friend. You go with Sam.*

It's your first varsity game and, although he's a solid player, you don't think throwing to Evan is the smartest play. You line up, do a beautiful flip throw, and send it to Darby. He jumps, rising above the Redmond defender, and loops his header over the Redmond goalkeeper. It's beautiful.

Since you haven't seen much action, you hope the scout noticed the precision of your toss. That would be something, but probably not enough. Then your chance comes. Jason crosses the ball to you. You dribble around three attackers with ease. You could keep moving, you want to – you want to take a shot and prove all your skills for the scout – but defenders are closing in, and you see Evan moving into prime position. You cross the ball to him. He powers toward the Redmond goal, crosses back to you. At the edge of the box, you get blocked and, before the ball is deflected, you pass to Jason. He barely tips it with his toe, but the redirect is enough that it gets by their goalie. The ref calls it over. You win!

After the game, someone taps you on the shoulder. It's the scout.

"I'm Mr. Murphy," he says, "and I like what I saw out there, number 7." He holds out a business card.

"Thank you," you say, shaking his hand.

"Coach Duncan from Weston told me that you were an aggressive dribbler. He said you're sometimes a one-man show, but I was impressed with the teamwork I saw today. That's what we're looking for on the Boys' National Team."

Go on to the next page.

He asks if you have any interest and you practically fall over with excitement. You can't believe how close you came to blowing it. For the first time, you realize that, even when you put the spotlight on others, you can still shine.

THE END

It's not that you don't want to practice with the girls – you know there's something to be said for finessing the ball – it's just that you'd rather focus on strength and speed right now, because you think that's what you'll need most to qualify for the Youth National Team in your age group. So, it's Saturday morning and you're going to run drills on your own instead of co-ed practice, where you would undoubtedly have to see Autumn.

Autumn. What are you going to do about Autumn? You pop a couple pieces of bread into the toaster and grab the butter and jelly from the fridge. Spinning the jar of jelly on the counter, you sigh audibly as you watch it turn round and round.

"As the jelly turns, so do the days of our lives," your dad says in his dorky announcer voice. You jump, surprised to find you're not alone, and catch the now tumbling jelly just before it flies off the counter. "Nice save," he continues. You force a laugh. "Hey, Kev, what's on your mind?" he asks. Fortunately, your mom comes in singing. She's always so happy in the morning.

"What are my guys up to today?" she asks, putting her arm around your shoulder.

"Uh, I'm just gonna run soccer drills and maybe head to the field later," you tell her.

"Okay, sweetie, just check in before you go. Oh, how's Autumn doing?" she asks.

You blurt out, "I don't know," sounding a little too defensive.

Go on to the next page.

You hope they won't ask more.

"How's Sam?" your dad asks your mom, and you breathe a sigh of relief.

"Much better," she says. "In fact, we're going to the DMV this morning, and I have no doubt she'll pass her driving test with flying colors."

You want to say something snide about her being a menace behind the wheel, but you know your parents won't appreciate your humor. Besides, you're just happy to have your mind on something other than confusing love. Then your mom walks over to your dad and you know what's coming next.

She walks up behind him, bends forward, and wraps her arms around his chest, putting her face next to his so that their cheeks are touching. It's this weird little thing they do every morning.

"I love you to the moon and back, Richie," she says.

"Jen, I love you twice that distance and more," he replies. Then they kiss.

"Ugh," you groan. "Do you guys have to do that in front of me?"

"Listen, buddy," your dad says, "when you find the person you want to be around every day, you never let them forget it."

"Fine," you shrug, shaking your head. So much for getting your mind off Autumn.

After a couple hours of drills, you're beat, and a little bored with being alone, so you decide to head down to the soccer field to check

Go on to the next page.

out the co-ed practice . . . just to see if you're missing anything.

Walking toward the clubhouse, you see a red truck with some guys from the Densen Soccer Club peeling out of the parking lot. You recognize Shawn Scarver. He's the only person who consistently steals the ball from you. It's not like you never lose the ball, but Shawn can always unstick your glue and it drives you crazy. What were *they* doing here?

The co-ed practice is ending. Autumn spots you and waves. She seems totally normal now, and even asks you to walk with her. "I'm sorry I acted so weird," she says. "I just didn't expect you to say that, but . . . " she hesitates, "it's cool, and, well, I was wondering if you'd go to the dance with me tomorrow."

You say yes, definitely.

Unfortunately, late the next day, Coach Duncan calls. He tells you that the championship trophy was stolen from his office. You know exactly who did it. *Of course that's why they were there.* The rivalry between Weston and Densen is legendary, and that trophy has been stolen a million times. You were so focused on Autumn, it hadn't even occurred to you. But what should you do now?

 GO TO **PAGE 23**. *You want to steal the trophy back, but that will make you late for the dance. You hope Autumn will understand.*

 GO TO **PAGE 32**. *You want to go get the trophy, but you don't want to blow your big chance with Autumn. You tell Coach Duncan, knowing he'll take care of it.*

You hope this won't be the only time the guys ask you to hang out with them, but you can't miss Bowie's birthday. Your best friend only turns 15 once.

In the car, Sam tells you she needs to pick up Joey first.

"Geeze, Sam," you complain. "I just gave up hanging out so I wouldn't be late."

"Chill, twerp. He's on the way." She eyes you for a minute, then her voice changes. "What's going on with you? Why so edgy?" It's her I-really-do-care big sister voice. She only uses it when she's being nice to you.

"I'm not," you start to deny, but then you end up spilling it all. You tell her you don't even know if Autumn still wants to be friends with you.

"Well, you can't really blame her for being mad," Sam suggests.

"I know," you concede, "I just needed Chuck to back off." You don't want to talk about it anymore, so you ask a random question. "Hey, why did you quit soccer for Joey?"

"What? Way to change the subject, and I didn't," she says. "I quit soccer because I want to run track." She raises her eyebrows at you. "You know, you shouldn't assume – it's better to ask. And as for Autumn, she'll come around. Tell her why you acted like such an idiot and apologize."

Sam's right; you need to talk to Autumn. You probably should have just done that in the first place, but there's no going back now, so you'll just have to see what happens.

THE END

You're worried that your parents won't even let you try out, because they won't want you to go abroad for soccer camp. They wouldn't let Sam go to Spain her freshman year, so why would they let you go to Holland?

Still, even if you went to the tryouts without permission and made it, are you going to sneak away to Holland too? You'll have to tell them, you just don't know how. Maybe Goda and Poppy can help.

You call and ask Poppy what he thinks. He suggests that you get prepared – have as much information as you can, and maybe even have your coach talk to them too.

"Now, tell me what's going on with your sweet friend, Autumn. Did you tell her how you feel?" he asks.

"Yeah," you say, "but it didn't go very well, and I think I've messed it up even more with another girl."

"Oh, son," he chuckles, "I'm sorry. It sounds like a real pickle."

You hear Goda in the background, scolding him for laughing, and demanding the phone.

"Kevin, honey?"

"Hi, Goda."

She wants all the details about what happened with Autumn and, even though you're embarrassed and don't really want to tell her everything, she gets it out of you.

Goda tells you to stop messing around with Katrina and talk to Autumn. You're just not sure Autumn will want to talk to you.

Go on to the next page.

When you hang up, your dad calls you to the living room.

"What's up, Dad?" you say as you enter the room.

"We heard you on the phone," he says. "It sounds like you might want to talk to us."

Oh, no, you're not prepared at all. This is not happening. "No, uh," you stutter, "um, I'm not ready yet."

"Look, if you need help talking to Autumn, we're here for you," your mom offers.

"Wait, what?" you say, confused.

"We heard you telling Goda and Poppy about things with Autumn," your dad says.

"Well, yeah, but that's not what I wanted to talk to you about."

"Oh, okay. Well, what did you want to talk to us about, then?"

"Well, um . . . " You're stuck now. "See, there's this soccer camp, and it's only for elite players, and there would be world-class coaches, and players from all over the world, and . . . "

"Okay, Kevin, get to it." Your dad interrupts you. "What *don't* you want to tell us?"

"Well," you sigh, "it's just that the camp is in, um, Holland."

At first they both say no – no way – but you keep your cool. Luckily, the camp is only two weeks long. They said no to Spain for Sam because it would have been three months, and they think 15 is too young to go away, let alone abroad, for that long.

"You know," your mom says, "it would show a lot of maturity if

Go on to the next page.

you were to talk with Autumn. That's the kind of maturity a world-travelling soccer player would exhibit."

"Aw, mom," you say, but you know that she and Goda are right.

The phone rings forever. Then, just before it goes to voicemail, Autumn picks up.

"I didn't think you were going to answer," you say.

"Neither did I."

"Listen, I just called to say I'm sorry," you offer.

"For what exactly?" She still sounds a little cold, but curious too.

"Well, you know."

"Say it," she challenges.

"I just," you stumble, "I'm sorry if I made you feel bad . . . or weird . . . or whatever. You're my best friend and I didn't mean to."

You're surprised and relieved that she forgives you almost immediately. You start to tell her about the soccer camp tryouts, but she already knows. She's trying out for the girls' team. You talk about the conditioning drills they'll have you do and how they'll look at your touch on the ball. You fall into an easy rhythm, a familiar space with someone you trust. She doesn't bring up the idea of being your girlfriend, and neither do you, but you know it's not the last time you'll talk about it. For now, you're going to focus on being a good best friend and getting to Holland for soccer camp.

THE END

You're flattered that Katrina wants to practice with you, but you really want to see if things are okay with Autumn. Laini even encourages you.

"Hey, Kevin," she says. "Autumn may be a little confused about some things right now, but she's not going to avoid you when it comes to playing soccer."

You tell Katrina no thanks. Still, a little part of you feels excited that she offered.

It doesn't matter though, because Laini was right; Autumn says she'll be your one-on-one partner. It's a great practice too. Autumn tells you that she's been working on her flip throw. She has the flip part down, since she's a gymnast, but her aim is inconsistent. You explain that it's how she's lining up for the flip and help her work on it. Somehow, over the course of the practice, it seems like things have gone back to normal. You think it might be just as well anyway. Maybe you're better as friends.

As Autumn lines up to do another flip throw, a ball comes out of nowhere and she gets beaned in the head. It practically knocks her off her feet. You grab for her as you look around to see where it came from. About 20 yards away, Katrina is waving at you.

"Sorry," she calls out.

"Oh my gosh," Laini yells as she runs over. She glares in Katrina's direction, "I can't believe she just did that! And right after your concussion from the car accident too."

Go on to the next page.

"Did what?" Autumn wants to know.

"Katrina likes Kevin and she aimed for your head," she says very matter-of-factly.

"What?" Autumn says, looking at you.

"What?" you echo. "She just offered to be my partner for practice."

"Nope, I saw it," Laini insists.

"That's messed up," Autumn says, rubbing her head.

Laini and Autumn start to get really mad at Katrina. They're ready to march over and confront her, but you're still not sure if it was intentional, so you offer to talk with her instead. Katrina seems a little high-energy and maybe even a bit mischievous, but outright mean? You're just not sure.

You're not sure of a lot right now. You're not sure if you should put all girlfriend thoughts of Autumn out of your head. You're not sure if you should *start* thinking about Katrina. You're not sure if coming to co-ed practice was the right choice. Here are the things you *are* sure of: Soccer is awesome, you will work crazy hard to get to the Olympics, and girls are really confusing.

THE END

You are super nervous to talk to Autumn, but she's been your friend your entire life, so what's the worst that can happen? Well, you guess the worst would be that she doesn't like you back, but there's only one way to find out. You try to look at the whole thing the way you'd look at a play for a game. Choose an appropriate formation to meet your opponent. Line up in position on the field. Execute. This situation requires a "change to attacking" formation, and the player you're going to sacrifice is Chuck.

You call Autumn and ask her to meet you at the park. She's sitting on one of the swings when you get there, gently kicking the ground and letting the swing carry her from side to side. She's got a slight smile on her face and looks as though she's lost in a daydream.

"Hey," you say as you walk up to her.

"Hey," she responds, snapping out of her daze.

You sit on the swing next to her, but you find it hard to make eye contact.

"Autumn," you begin, "we've been friends for a really long time, and, um, well, can I tell you something?" you say awkwardly, then change it, "I mean, ask you something?"

"Yeah, weirdo, you can tell or ask me anything," she says, laughing lightly.

"Well, I was wondering about Chuck," you say, "I noticed that he was, I don't know, you know, kinda flirting with you."

"What?" she laughs, "Are you crazy? He's a senior."

Go on to the next page.

"What if he did . . . you know, like you?" you ask.

"Wait," she says, planting her feet on the ground, "Did he say he likes me?"

Great, now you're Chuck's wing man. This is not going well at all.

"No, no," you say, trying to regain control of the conversation. "I just think he's kinda creepy to flirt with you. I mean, he's almost 18." She just shakes her head, like what you're saying doesn't make sense. "Besides," you go on, "I think I like you."

"What?" she says. "You think *you* like me?" Now she's standing with her hands on her hips. "What does that even mean, 'you *think* you like me?' Why were you talking about Chuck then? And when did you start thinking you like me?" She's firing questions faster than your brain can take them in, and you don't know what to say. You didn't know how this would go, but you definitely didn't imagine it going like this.

"I do like you," you say. "I do." Now you're standing too. You still can't look her in the eye, but you see the look on her face change, like she's realized something. Suddenly, she starts crying.

"This is just . . . I just . . . you're my best friend," she says, and with that, she turns and runs away. At first, you want to run after her, but your feet feel like they're cemented to the ground and your stomach is churning. You just sit back down on the swing and stare at the ground.

That night, you try calling Autumn three or four times, but her

Go on to the next page.

phone just goes to voicemail. Then, the next morning, she doesn't show up to walk with you, so you ask Sam for a ride.

Joey usually picks up Sam with his sister, Meghan, and her boyfriend, Evan, who also happens to be on the soccer team with you. Evan is calm, focused, and soft spoken, unlike Chuck, who sounds like a WWF wrestler. He's been really nice to you, and didn't even join in on the "kid" jokes at practice. You like Evan.

In the car, he confides in you that he feels like some of the guys block him out in favor of the other forwards so, even though he gets out on the field, he doesn't often get an opportunity to shine. You think that stinks and wish you could help. Who knew your chance would come so soon?

It's your first varsity game, and there's a scout for the Boys' National Team. Coach says he wants to see what you've got, so he starts you, but you don't see much action. At the beginning of the second half, one of the Redmond attackers boots it out over a sideline. You grab the ball and back up for your legendary flip throw. Scanning the field, you see that Evan is open, but so is Darby. You really want to make the right call. What should you do?

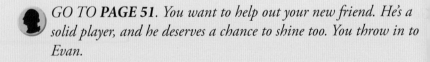

GO TO **PAGE 51**. *You want to help out your new friend. He's a solid player, and he deserves a chance to shine too. You throw in to Evan.*

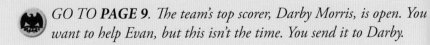

GO TO **PAGE 9**. *The team's top scorer, Darby Morris, is open. You want to help Evan, but this isn't the time. You send it to Darby.*

You can't believe Shawn Scarver and his crew stole the trophy right in front of you. You don't mention anything to Coach Duncan, because *you're* going to get it back. Now, you just need to make a plan. First, you have to call Autumn. Maybe she'll want to blow off the dance and come with you.

Autumn's mom answers her mobile phone.

"Oooh, hi, Kevin," she says, sounding ridiculously excited. "Are you getting ready for the dance?"

"Um, yeah," you lie. "Um, could I please talk to Autumn?"

"One minute, sweetie, she's curling her hair."

Curling her hair? Since when does Autumn curl her hair? This is not a good sign. You don't think she's going to want to come, and now you're wondering if you should even tell her what's going on.

"Hey, Kev, I'm so psyched for tonight. What's up?"

"I, uh, I," you trip over your words, "I have to meet you there," you manage.

"Oh," she says sounding disappointed. "Well, how come? Is everything okay?"

"Yeah, no," you say, *which isn't confusing at all*. Then try to make up for it. "Um, yeah, it's just that Sam's driving and she has some errand to run before we can go."

She accepts your lame excuse, but sounds pretty bummed. You hate lying to her, but you can tell that she's really into the dance, and you don't think the mission will go too late.

Go on to the next page.

Now, you need a team to help execute the retrieval mission. Of course, you call Bowie first.

"Hey, Bowie man, how's it going?"

"Hey, Kev. How are you?"

"Well, first of all, were you planning on going to the dance tonight?"

"There's a dance?" he says.

"Okay, perfect. Listen, I'm putting together a team to retrieve a stolen item. It's very valuable, and there may be some danger. You in?"

"A real mission?" he asks. "Of course I am. I have some new gadgets too."

"Sweet," you say. "Well, gather together anything that could be useful for retrieval and I'll be over in a little bit. I just have to find us a ride."

Now, who can be your driver? Sam's out. She's definitely going to the dance, and you just hope she doesn't get there earlier than you. Normally, she and her friends meet up before dances so they can all get ready together. It takes forever and they're never on time. You know this, because sometimes you're unlucky enough to have them all gather at your house. The only other person who's not a grown-up – but has access to wheels – is Joey, Sam's boyfriend. Hopefully he doesn't have anything else going on while he waits to meet up with Sam and her friends.

Go on to the next page.

Joey jumps at the idea. He's pretty crazy, so tracking down a stolen trophy, possibly breaking into someone's house, and retrieving the trophy sounds like a lot of fun to him.

You pack a bag with your clothes for the dance, a flashlight, and your army knife. Joey meets you down the street, so as not to raise any suspicion, and you sneak out by telling your parents that you'll get ready at Autumn's. They are as ridiculously giddy as her mom about you two going to a dumb dance, so you use it to your advantage.

When you get in the car, Joey does his signature hair-toss introduction of himself, but instead of yelling "Jo-aaay," he whispers it, and says he's being covert. You crack up, feeling very lucky that your sister has such a cool boyfriend. You also feel lucky that Bowie is a master inventor.

He has a mechanical arm that looks like it can extend at least three feet, with articulating metal fingers. Each finger has a rubber pad attached to the tip, which Bowie explains is for gripping things better. He also has a small remote-control robot with a camera that syncs up to his phone. You feel like an international spy whenever you play with him. Joey is in heaven too.

"Okay, guys, here's the plan" you say, once you're all in the car. "I'm positive the trophy will be at Shawn's house, because his dad is the coach of the Densen club." They both nod. "I've been in his house before, and they have a huge trophy case in the front room. Only problem is that, if they're home, we'll have to abort our mission."

Go on to the next page.

The house is empty and the skylight is open. The trophy is exactly where you thought it would be. Could it get any easier? You and Joey climb onto the roof and Bowie instructs you on how to use the mechanical arm, but it's just not long enough. Joey gets the idea to lower you down so you can grab the trophy. It seems like a good idea until it isn't, and it isn't as soon as you're dangling four feet above Shawn's living room floor and Joey accidentally drops you.

You instinctually put your hands out, which breaks your fall, but also badly tweaks your right wrist. You muffle a cry of pain, and you hope the thud wasn't too loud. Joey whispers apologies from above as you cradle your sore arm to your chest. You grab the trophy and head for the door. Mission accomplished.

You're half an hour late for the dance. You expect to see Autumn sitting alone in a corner, and you're fully prepared to offer massive apologies and regale her with the story of your heroism. But, she's not alone at all. In fact, she's dancing with Chuck Grady, the keeper for the varsity soccer team, and he's a senior. What just happened? There's a senior dancing with the girl you like, you've got a sprained wrist, which means no flip throws, and you went from hero to zero in seconds flat. This is not where you saw the evening going. Sure you got the trophy back, but you'd do it all differently if you could choose again.

THE END

You can't believe you have to choose between your soccer club and playing on the varsity team your first year in high school. Your gut is telling you to stay with your club. Not only have you been there forever, but Coach Duncan knows your dream to play in the Olympics and he's dedicated to helping you achieve it. Plus, he's an amazing coach.

Just after school on your first day, Coach Oliver, calls. You know it's him, because you recognize the number from the high school on the phone display. You don't answer it.

Instead, you listen to the message he leaves. Actually, you listen to the message three times. Then you finally call Coach Duncan from Weston. When you tell him about the offer to play varsity, his first reaction is to talk you out of it, but then he says that you need to do what you want. He tells you there's many ways to achieve your dream. You tell him you're happy with Weston and he's glad you're going to stay. You wish you could call Autumn right now, but you're still nervous about talking to her.

Instead, you make the difficult call to Coach Oliver. He's disappointed, but understands, and he still invites you to swing by a practice sometime. He says you never know what can happen over the next four years.

Okay, now that that's figured out, what are you going to do about Autumn? She's your best friend. Maybe you should just ignore your new feelings for her. That might be easier than telling her you like

Go on to the next page.

her. You don't want her to laugh in your face, and you don't want to wreck your friendship with her or with Bowie. The three of you do almost everything together, except play soccer. Bowie is more of a scientist than an athlete, but even he gets into the game. He once used physics to help you advance a move that was giving you trouble, and, even though you don't know how he gets his machines to work, you love helping him test them. Autumn is both smart and athletic, which makes her the perfect third in your trio. She can challenge you any day on the field, and she can understand most of Bowie's mad scientist creations. You don't want to mess up what you all have together.

You are lying on your bed thinking about what to do when you hear the doorbell ring. It's your Goda and Poppy, your mom's parents. When you were little, you said "go-da" instead of "grand-ma", but you're not sure why, that's just what your mouth did with the word. Everyone thought it was cute, so it stuck.

You tell them about Sam hitting Autumn with the car, and your big decision between Weston and the varsity team. Then, somehow, it slips out that you're feeling weird about Autumn.

"Do you mean you like her?" Goda asks. You shrug and Poppy chuckles.

"When I first told your grandma I liked her, I was so nervous," Poppy offers, "but I believe in being up-front."

After practice the next day, you walk across to the adjoining field

Go on to the next page.

where the girls are running drills. When they're finished, you take Autumn aside. Although you try to say it casually, you just sort of blurt out that you like her. It's pretty awkward. She looks at you like you've lost your mind, then gets kind of mad, then starts to cry. Then she runs over by her girlfriends and won't even look at you. How confusing.

That's when Coach Duncan comes over with the rest of your team. He calls all the girls over and let's everyone know he's offering an optional co-ed practice on Saturdays. He says you can learn from each other, because boys tend to use strength and speed more, while girls are usually better at technique and finessing the ball. This is a tricky decision.

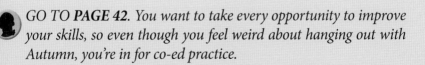

*GO TO **PAGE 42**. You want to take every opportunity to improve your skills, so even though you feel weird about hanging out with Autumn, you're in for co-ed practice.*

*GO TO **PAGE 11**. You want to focus on strength and speed to contend with aggressive players. You opt out of co-ed practice.*

You're grateful to have a friend on the team, especially since Chuck isn't too happy with you for lying to him about Autumn, but you just don't think that helping Evan improve his game is the best way to improve yours. Not only are you about to play your first game as a varsity team member, but it will be in front of a scout for the Boys' National Team. You need to focus on your own game and get ready for that scout.

You decide to call Coach Duncan from the Weston Soccer Club for some advice on how to train. You hope he won't mind hearing from you after you decided to leave the club for a chance to play varsity, and you're in luck. He's actually happy you called.

"I have some great news," he tells you.

"Hey, me too, Coach," you say.

"Okay, you first," he says

"We've got a scout from the Boys' National Team coming to our first game."

"That's great, Kevin, but I'm not surprised," coach says, laughing. "he's coming into town to meet me and check out the club."

"Oh," is all you manage to say, feeling a bit deflated.

Coach Duncan can tell you're disappointed, so he changes the subject and asks how you'll get ready for the scout. You tell him that's why you called, and he suggests you focus on your long pass.

"Set up a target about 20 feet from you," he says, "then, kick the ball into the air; when it comes down, control and pass it to the target. Do this drill, and you'll improve your aim. And, Kevin," he adds, "you'll impress him. You're a freshman playing varsity, so he's already going to be interested in you. Just focus and remember to share the ball."

Between team practice and running drills on your own, you're feeling good come game day. The stands are filled. You see your parents and grandparents. Even Sam is here. Bowie would have been, but today's his birthday and he went to the city with his parents. The only person missing is Autumn. She's never missed a game before, unless she had one of her own, of course, but that was when you were friends. You guess that's over now.

Coach Oliver starts you, and things are going pretty well. Only, these guys are big. They're stronger and more aggressive than what you're used to, and when you challenge a Redmond player for the ball, you get knocked down. That's normal enough, but the force of the knockdown is powerful, and you put your arm out to brace yourself. Your wrist gets twisted. The ball goes out over the sideline, so the throw-in is yours. Your wrist isn't broken, but it hurts, and this is definitely going to affect your flip throw. Is it worth it?

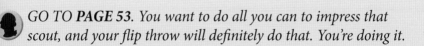

GO TO **PAGE 53**. *You want to do all you can to impress that scout, and your flip throw will definitely do that. You're doing it.*

GO TO **PAGE 7**. *It's not worth the risk of injuring yourself further. You know you'll impress him with your control of the ball and your dribbling skills. You do a regular throw-in.*

You know it must have been Shawn and his buddies who took the trophy, and you really want to go get it back, but this dance is your big chance with Autumn. You tell Coach Duncan what you saw. You're relieved when he says he'll take care of it.

Then there's a knock on your bedroom door.

"I've got a little something for you," your mom says as she comes into your room. "It's downstairs in the fridge."

"What?" you ask.

"Kevin," she says in a disapproving voice, when she sees you sprawled out on your bed. "The dance is in an hour. Don't you think you should get in the shower? And what are you going to wear?"

"I was just waiting for Sam to get out," you say.

"Sam got out of the shower ten minutes ago and went to Diane's. Here," she says, pulling a blue button-up shirt from your closet, "this will look nice with pants and a belt."

"No way. Too formal. People will make fun of me."

After you complain for another five minutes, she compromises. You can wear your favorite T-shirt. It says "Messi Rules" – you think he's the best Brazilian player there ever was. But you can only wear it *under* your button-up, and you have to wear pants, not jeans.

"Hey, you said you had something for me," you wonder out loud.

"Oh, yes," she says, brightening up. "I got you a corsage for Autumn."

"A what?" you ask.

Go on to the next page.

"A corsage, silly. For her wrist. Now, Autumn's dress is blue, so I got you a white orchid with little bluebell accent flowers."

"Whatever, mom," you say, rolling your eyes. Like you care what kind of flowers she got. "Um, thanks," you add, when you see her shoulders slump in disappointment.

"No problem," she shrugs. "Oh, and Sam will be back by six to get you, so hop in the shower," she says, scooting you toward the door.

You've been to Autumn's house a million times, but this is different somehow. You're nervous, and you walk up to her door one slow step at a time. Before you knock, the door bursts open and Autumn's mom practically throws you into the house, saying she needs to get pictures, lots of pictures. Then you see Autumn. Her long brown hair is down, and she's curled it. You think she might be wearing a little makeup. You want to ask who she is and what she's done with your best friend, but you're a bit tongue-tied. She looks beautiful.

After a thousand or so pictures, you finally leave for the dance. It's actually pretty fun. You and Autumn slip into your familiar friendship mode and dance like crazy people. But then a slow song comes on. At first you just stand there frozen. The blood drains from your face and you feel a little faint. Then, Chuck Grady, a senior and the keeper for the varsity soccer team, walks up to Autumn. *Is he going to ask her to dance?* You don't wait to find out. You pull her onto the dance floor. You're a little awkward at slow dancing, but she doesn't seem to mind.

THE END

You can't believe the seniors asked you to hang out with them. You feel bad about being late for Bowie's birthday dinner, but you can't pass up this opportunity. You send him a quick text, and tell Sam that you'll catch a ride with one of the guys.

Back out at the bleachers, all the spectators have gone. A few of the guys are there playing hacky-sack and talking about the game.

"Hey, the kid looks thirsty," Jason says. "Give him a beer."

Chuck tosses you a can. You don't drink, but you don't want to be "the kid" to them all year.

While they toss back beer after beer, you slowly sip yours and hope no one will notice. Luckily, they don't. Then, they run out and want to get more. You need to get to Bowie's anyway. Chuck, who has probably had the most to drink, offers you a ride. This is not good.

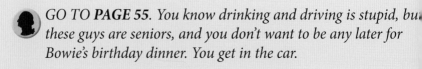 GO TO **PAGE 55**. *You know drinking and driving is stupid, but these guys are seniors, and you don't want to be any later for Bowie's birthday dinner. You get in the car.*

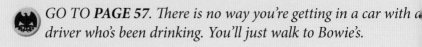 GO TO **PAGE 57**. *There is no way you're getting in a car with a driver who's been drinking. You'll just walk to Bowie's.*

Autumn has been so weird since you told her you like her, and even though you'd rather practice with her, and Laini assures you she would say yes if you asked, you decide to take Katrina up on her offer. Katrina seems cool, and you're too nervous to try talking to Autumn again just yet.

While you practice one-on-one with Katrina, you keep stealing glances at Autumn, but she won't even look at you. There's not much you can do right now, so you decide to just focus on practice.

Katrina is actually really good. She can even pull off a quality Elastico dribbling move. You ask her to go over it with you, and promise to give her some pointers on stealing.

"Okay," she says, positioning herself next to you. "Start with the ball close, then push it slightly forward and sideways, with the outside of your foot."

You start to make the move, but she giggles and grabs you by the waist, pulling you back.

"Now just wait a minute," she says, giggling again. "I wasn't finished."

"Oh, sorry," you say and try to back away from her a little. It was kind of weird the way she grabbed you.

"So," she continues, "after you push it forward and sideways, quickly cut it in the opposite direction." She demonstrates and finishes, "Just make sure you use the same foot, but with the inside, when you redirect."

Go on to the next page.

Huntington City
Township Public Library
255 West Park Drive
Huntington, IN 46750

"Got it, thanks," you say.

Katrina seems cool, but a little pushy. You really wish you could go talk to Autumn.

At the end of practice, you look around for Autumn, but she's gone before you know it. Katrina, on the other hand, doesn't want to leave you alone. She stands over you while you pack up your things. She says you should hang out more. She even grabs your phone and puts her number in it. Luckily, Coach Duncan calls you over, so you quickly thank her for practice and escape. Coach tells you about an amazing opportunity.

There's an international soccer camp, run by the Development Academy, for Under-15 players. It's for truly elite players only. He says you'll have to try out, because they only take 18 boys, but he has high hopes you'll make it. The only thing he has a concern about is that the camp is in Holland. He offers to call your parents, but you ask him not to, because you want to talk to them first. There may be a problem.

During her freshman year, Sam wanted to go to Spain for a semester abroad. She had been working extra babysitting hours, she'd been studying Spanish every night, and she even put together a PowerPoint presentation to make her case for why it would be the most enriching, amazing experience of her life. But, even after all of that, your parents still said no. They thought it was too big of a trip for a freshman. What's to make them change their minds for you?

Go on to the next page.

When you get home you head into your room to formulate a plan. Normally, at a time like this, you'd call Autumn, but since that's not an option, and Bowie wasn't very helpful with your last soccer decision, you use the new number in your phone, and see what Katrina thinks.

"Wow, I didn't think you'd call," is the first thing she says.

"Well," you laugh, "I did."

"Yeah, I got that," she giggles. "So, what's up?"

You tell her all about the camp in Holland and how you really want to go. You tell her about your dream to compete in the Olympics too. Then, you explain what happened when Sam wanted to go to Spain.

"You know," she says, sounding like she's got an idea, "I'm always in favor of asking for forgiveness instead of permission."

"What do you mean?" you ask.

"Well, what if we snuck out and took the bus to Clayton? We could both try out. And, when you inevitably get chosen, your parents will have to let you go."

It sounds risky, but it's not the worst idea ever. You're just not sure what to do.

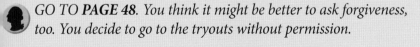

GO TO **PAGE 48**. *You think it might be better to ask forgiveness, too. You decide to go to the tryouts without permission.*

GO TO **PAGE 15**. *Katrina's proposal is tempting, but why even bother going to the tryouts if they're not going to let you go in the end? You tell them and hope for the best.*

You can't believe you're choosing between your soccer club and playing on the varsity team your first year in high school. Part of you feels like you should stay with your club. In general, the play is more competitive among the soccer clubs. Plus, how can you leave Coach Duncan? He's been there for you, and he wants to help you achieve your dream of the Olympics. But playing varsity as a freshman is such an amazing opportunity.

You can't pass it up. You'll get to play with really talented players – All-State players – who have years more experience than you, and you'll definitely learn a ton. Plus, as a new kid going into high school, it might be nice to have some older friends . . . assuming your teammates like you, of course. It will be difficult to leave Weston, but playing for the high school varsity team is the right choice for you.

Just after school on your first day, Coach Oliver calls. You know it's him, because you recognize the number from the high school on the phone display.

"Hello? Coach Oliver?" you say, sounding a bit more enthusiastic than you meant to.

"Hi," he says, a little confused. "Is this Kevin Faklaw?"

"Yup. That's me."

"Well, Kevin, I get the feeling you already know why I'm calling, but let me go ahead and ask you anyway. Would you be interested in playing on the varsity team this year? There might even be a chance you could start," he says.

Go on to the next page.

"Yeah, yeah definitely," you say, still finding it hard to believe this is happening. "Coach Oliver, I really want to make the U.S. Soccer Boys' National Team," you admit. "And I want to go to the Olympics."

"Well, then I guess you'll be happy to hear that we've got a scout from the Boys' National Team coming to our first game," he says.

"No way!" You can't believe it.

"You bet. And I'm glad to hear you're so dedicated, Kevin, because I don't offer a varsity spot to a freshman every day. In fact," he says, "you'll be the first."

Coach Oliver isn't worried about you being accepted by the other players, because he knows you have the talent to gain their respect. Still, he points out that even with your skills, competing against players two, three, or even four years older will sometimes be difficult. Plus, he warns, you'll have to deal with all the other challenges of high school life, and maintain at least a "B" average. He wants to know if you're up for it.

"Yes, sir," you assure him, and he tells you to be at practice tomorrow after school.

Now you just have to call Coach Duncan and tell him about your decision.

"Kevin," he says, "I know this is an exciting opportunity for a freshman, and the Darrington High School team is an excellent team, but you do understand that you won't play with the club at all this season, right?"

Go on to the next page.

"I know, Coach."

"And you know it means less game time throughout the year? He's not telling you "don't do it," but he may as well be."

"I know, Coach," you say, hating that you're disappointing him.

"Well, I guess you have to do what's best for you, but I'm really sad to see you go."

Then you get an idea.

"Hey, Coach," you say, "could I just *practice* with the club in the spring?"

"Hmmm," he says, considering it. "I suppose, if you want to train with us after your high school season is over, I'll let you."

You suddenly feel like you just got every gift you asked for on your birthday.

At your first varsity practice, you get a pretty good sense of what it will be like to play with upper classmen – they're bigger, stronger, faster, and more aggressive than the guys you've been playing with – but you are determined to hold your own.

"Now, I know you can dribble," Coach Oliver says to you. "But I want you to save it for the attacking third of the field. If you lose the ball there, our opposition is less likely to find a goal-scoring opportunity. If you hold onto it and get past the defender, there's a better chance *we'll* find a goal-scoring opportunity."

You nod in agreement, and he asks how you feel about your defensive skills. You tell him that you know how to support

Go on to the next page.

defenders, but you'd welcome some practice. Coach Oliver pairs you with Deacon for some one-on-one; he's a Junior who keeps the ball under close control and you're excited to learn from him.

As practice wraps up, Coach Oliver reminds everyone that there's a scout coming to your first game. He tells you Mr. Murphy will be looking for players to compete in different age groups of the U.S. Soccer Boys' National Team.

You still can't believe it. You're going to get to play for a scout at your first varsity game. There's a good chance Coach Oliver will let you start, and you're planning to get out there and show Mr. Murphy exactly why he should choose you.

While talking with Coach Oliver about the scout, you notice Autumn walking over. She must be here to see how your first varsity practice went. Then you notice the goalie, Chuck Grady, walking over to her. He starts talking to her. That's really weird. Why is *he* talking to Autumn? Does she know him? He's a senior. Even though you haven't figured out how to tell her you like her, or if you even should, she's still your best friend, and this is not cool.

You excuse yourself from Coach Oliver and, as you get closer to them, you realize that he's not just talking to her, he's *flirting* with her! Well, this is just great. Now, not only do you have secret feelings for Autumn, but you're also jealous. You have to do something about this.

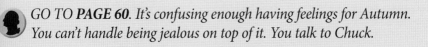

GO TO **PAGE 60**. *It's confusing enough having feelings for Autumn. You can't handle being jealous on top of it. You talk to Chuck.*

GO TO **PAGE 20**. *Autumn has been your best friend forever. You just need to talk to her and tell her how you feel. What's the worst that can happen?*

Coach thinks that playing with the girls will help you and the other boys improve your technical skills. You're open to any opportunity to improve your skills, so co-ed weekend practice seems like a great idea. Well, all except for the part where you have to see Autumn. You wish she hadn't been so weird when you told her you like her.

On Friday nights, you would normally do something with Autumn and Bowie. Sometimes you go to the movies; sometimes you play video games; sometimes, you just play with Bowie's gadgets and dream up international spy adventures where you could use them. Tomorrow is Bowie's birthday though, so this Friday, you, Goda and Poppy are coming over to help you with his gift.

Both your grandparents are artists. Poppy is a wood carver and a welder. He makes the coolest sculptures. Goda is a painter. She's also really good at building and refinishing things. And when they combine their talents, they can do anything. They're helping you make a toolbox. Bowie's work area is always such a mess, and he can never find his tools. You secretly cataloged his things and Goda helped you design a box that would fit all his tools. Poppy has been helping you cut and sand the pieces, as well as assemble them, and tonight you're going to finish and paint it.

Aside from your abilities on the soccer field, you've never been so proud of anything before. You even carved the handle (with your Poppy's help, of course). There are two trays that lift out of the top to easily access the smaller tools in them, as well as the larger tools

Go on to the next page.

below, and there's a drawer in the bottom. It is the coolest toolbox ever made. You can't wait to give it to Bowie tomorrow at his birthday dinner. Now, if you can just avoid Autumn at co-ed practice, you'll only have to survive seeing her at the dinner.

Coach Duncan starts with some drills, and then it's time to scrimmage. You figure it'll be boys against girls, but he mixes the teams. Of course, Autumn ends up on your team. It's been a long time since you've actually played on a team together. Dinking around doing one-on-one drills, which is what you usually do, doesn't really count. You're really impressed with her game. She holds onto the ball, and her short passes have come a long way. It's a great scrimmage, and it ends in a tie with one goal each.

After the scrimmage, Coach Duncan says he's going to pair you all up – one boy, one girl. You really *don't* want to avoid Autumn, but you're not even sure if she's talking to you. Maybe it would be best to ask her friend, Laini. You walk over and tap her on the shoulder.

"Hey, how's it going, Laini?"

"I'm alright, lover-boy," she teases. "How are you?"

"Great, so Autumn told you?" you ask.

"Duh, of course she did."

"Well, that's kinda what I wanted to talk about. I want to ask her to practice with me, but I don't know if she's talking to me."

"I'd be your partner," a pretty red-head says, tossing you a ball.

"Oh, uh, hi," you say, a little confused.

Go on to the next page.

"I'm Katrina, what's your name?"

"Uh, Kevin," you say.

"Well, *Uh*-Kevin, you want to be my partner for the drill?" sh smiles.

"I . . . " you hesitate.

"He already has a partner," Laini answers for you, leering a Katrina.

"That's not what *I* heard him say," Katrina fires back.

This is getting ugly fast. You need to make a decision.

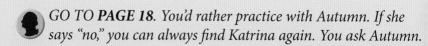

GO TO **PAGE 18**. *You'd rather practice with Autumn. If she says "no," you can always find Katrina again. You ask Autumn.*

GO TO **PAGE 35**. *You saw Katrina juggling, so you know she has skills. Plus, you're too nervous to find out if Autumn is even speaking to you. You partner with Katrina.*

You are very grateful to Evan. He's the only one who didn't make any "kid" jokes about you. He also looks up to you, even though he's older, which makes you feel good. It doesn't hurt that you could really use a friend right now either. So, you tell him you'd be happy to spend some extra time practicing with him.

You've never really been in a coaching-type situation before. Well, except for the time Coach Duncan had you all mentor the nine-year-olds, but that was super simple. This is like real coaching. You know that Evan's weakness is that he sometimes forgets to look up, which is why you're able to snag the ball. You come up with some techniques to help him control the ball while not looking at it.

Evan is grateful to you for helping him. The thing is, though, you've found that by paying close attention to his technique, it's actually teaching you about your own. If you hadn't worked with him on ball control, you wouldn't have realized that you have a certain body-movement "tell" every time you're going to do a Cruyff, or cut back, maneuver. Evan noticed it while you were teaching him the move. He said that every time you're going to chop the ball behind you, your "fake" shooting leg lifts higher than it would if you were really going to take a shot. This whole thing has been as helpful for you as it has been for him. Win-win.

You and Evan have trained together after every practice this week, and you're feeling good about your first varsity game on Saturday.

"If we keep going like this, they'll think we can read each other's

Go on to the next page.

minds," you laugh.

"No doubt," Evan chuckles. "Our passes will be legendary."

You usually pride yourself on doing it all, but begin to realize that it would be amazing to have a partner on the field like that – to pass through narrow holes and get by the most determined defense. That would be cool.

"I'm so psyched there's going to be a scout there," you say, thinking about your plans for playing soccer in the Olympics.

"So, you want to play for the Boys' National Team, huh?" he asks.

"Heck, yeah," you say. "I'm going to the Olympics."

"That's cool, man," Evan says, and then gets a funny look on his face. "You know, my uncle is actually a trainer at the Olympic prep soccer camp."

"What?!" You can't believe it. "Are you serious?"

You want to know why the heck he doesn't train with his uncle. Evan explains that he's just not good enough. He says his uncle works with him sometimes, but the camp is for truly elite players. Evan says he'll introduce you. He thinks you'll be a good fit.

This is incredible – you feel like you could go through the roof you're so pumped.

"Oh, man, I have no idea how to repay you for this," you say.

"Hey, no worries," he says. "You totally deserve it. Why do you think I asked you to practice with me?" he asks rhetorically. "You're really good. I know you practice hard. It shows. But you have some

Go on to the next page.

serious natural talent. It's cool that you want to use it to go places."
He shrugs, "And I'm happy to help. Let's just call it payback for you
helping me."

"Well, I feel like I should do something," you say. "Do you want
to go see the new Spider-Man movie with me and my buddy, Bowie,
tonight?"

"Sure, sounds good," he says.

You all meet at the theater at six o'clock. Bowie and Evan get
along great, and you almost forget for a moment that the real third to
your trio is missing. It's not long before you start thinking of Autumn
though. You don't know what you'll do to make it up to her. How can
everything be so great and such a mess at the same time?

THE END

Katrina thinks it's better to ask for forgiveness than permission. She thinks you two should sneak out, take the bus to Clayton, and try out for the international soccer camp. Her theory is that if you make the cut, your parents will have to let you train in Holland. Seems like a good plan to you.

"Okay," you say. "We have to get the bus schedule."

"I'm already looking up the bus schedule online," she says. "Maybe you can call Coach to see if we need anything else."

You agree to and tell her you'll call her back later, after your friend Bowie's birthday dinner.

The first thing she asks about when you call is if you saw Autumn. Of course you did, since she's best friends with Bowie too, but why does Katrina care? Then she wants to know what you talked about. *Boy, is she pushy.* You change the subject to the tryouts, but now you can't stop thinking about how Autumn completely ignored you at dinner. Luckily, Bowie didn't seem to notice anything. You still haven't figured out how to tell him. You're not even sure what's going on with Autumn anymore, but you do know that you want to go to those tryouts.

You make a plan to meet Katrina at the bus station tomorrow evening at five. She tells you the bus will cost 12 dollars, and you remind her to bring warm clothes for the walk from the station in Clayton to the convention center. It all feels very covert and exciting.

All day Sunday, you waver between feeling anxious and eager.

Go on to the next page.

You avoid conversations with your parents, because they usually catch you when you're up to something. You focus on training.

It's about a half-hour walk to the bus station from your house, so you pack your bag and head out the door at four thirty. You tell your parents that you're headed to the library to do homework with Bowie. Well, really you shout it to them as you run out the door, so that they can't ask any questions. You've got your gear, your money for the bus, and you are jumping out of your skin with anticipation. You're sneaking away to an international soccer camp tryout. This is so cool.

Katrina is at the station waiting, and she already has your ticket. You offer to pay her back, but she doesn't want your money. She tells you it's a gift.

On the bus, Katrina starts asking about Autumn again. You wish she would let it go, but she seems determined to know how you feel about her and what's going on with you two. You tell her what happened and she says it's Autumn's loss. She says you should forget about her and just focus on your soccer goals. She says she'll be a better supporter for you than Autumn ever could. Just look at what she did for you tonight.

When the bus stops at a gas station, a bunch of people go in and use the bathroom. You ask Katrina if she wants anything, and she asks for bottled water and a granola bar. You check your watch. You'll be in Clayton with plenty of time to spare.

Go on to the next page.

While you're paying, the woman behind you yells, *"Gun!"* She's pointing at a man to your right. The door is to your left. For a moment, you consider running for it, but he draws his gun and tells everyone to stay put.

He makes everyone get down and clears the register. The guy behind the counter keeps saying he doesn't want trouble. There is a woman sobbing. You feel the hair on your arms sticking up and your whole body stiffens. You hope Katrina is still outside on the bus.

Finally, the man gets all the money and takes off. Everyone is okay. Then, the police show up to take statements. As if all of this isn't bad enough, one of the cops is Detective Hughes, a friend of your dad. Now you've been held at gunpoint, you're busted, and you'll never make it to the tryouts. What else could happen?

"I'm so glad you're okay," Katrina says, running up to you with tears in her eyes. She tells you they saw the whole thing from the bus, and about 10 people called the police. Then she kisses you. Her lips are soft and warm, and she smells sweet, like oranges. You don't know what you're going to do about missing the tryouts, or getting busted for taking the bus without permission, or even what you're going to do about Autumn, but for that one moment, nothing else seems to matter.

THE END

There are two plays you can make. The sure one, where you throw out to Darby, your team's top scorer, or you take a risk on your new friend, Evan. You know he really wants a chance to shine, and he seems to be a pretty solid player, so you trust him to make the right move when he gets the ball. You toss out to Evan.

He leans back slightly, puts his arms out, and controls the ball with his chest. There's no one close enough to challenge him. Nobody expected you to mark Evan; they were all ready to pounce on Darby. This is perfect. It gives Evan just enough time to control the ball, set it out in front of himself, and make a wicked instep shot that soars right past the Redmond team's unsuspecting goalie to the back of the net. Fantastic!

The Redmond team is super aggressive, but you get another opportunity to show that you can maneuver around them and, even though they ultimately win the game, you walk away with two assists and the confidence that you can hang with the upperclassmen on the field.

After the game, while the guys are all congratulating Evan on his sweet shot, Mr. Murphy, the scout, and Coach Oliver tell you they were impressed with you out there today.

"Faklaw," Darby says, walking up to you, "that was a genius call you made, throwing out to Evan. No one saw it coming."

"Uh, thanks," you say. You don't mind that one of the team's best players thinks you're a strategic mastermind, and if Mr. Murphy gets

Go on to the next page.

that idea too, it would be fine with you.

Just then, someone calls your name. It's Autumn. You're not really sure what to say or do.

"Hey," she says, kicking the grass nervously. "Um, I'm sorry for freaking out yesterday, and, well, uh, I . . . I really care about you."

"Nice to see you again, Autumn," Chuck yells over to her. Autumn smiles at him and you think you see her blush a little. Then she says she'll always be your friend, but she's not sure about the rest. She just wanted to make sure things weren't weird between you two for Bowie's birthday dinner. She says she'll see you there and walks away.

"So what's the deal, Faklaw?" Is she your girl or what?" Chuck wants to know.

"I dunno," you say, wishing he would just back off. Then he surprises you.

"You want her to be, don't you?" he asks, sounding sympathetic.

"Yeah, I guess so," you admit.

"Well, I'm not gonna get in your way, dude. There are plenty of pretty girls around."

Chuck shrugs his shoulders and turns away. You can't believe it. The only problem now is, what if Autumn actually does like Chuck? Well, you can't worry about that tonight. Who she does or doesn't like will have to be tomorrow's problem.

THE END

You want to do all you can to impress the scout, and your precision flip throw is a money maker, because you can cover distance and hit your mark. Unfortunately, your wrist is really sore from twisting it. You don't care though – you want to show the scout everything you've got. You'll show him this, then wow him with your offensive moves.

You grab the ball and move about 15 feet from the touch line. You scan the field. Darby's open. You line up, burst forward about three steps, hurling yourself upside-down. You plant the ball and flip your legs up over your head. Normally, this is when your feet would hit the ground, you'd release the ball, and it would shoot to your mark. Not today though.

When you plant the ball, your injured wrist buckles. You hear something snap, and pain shoots through your arm. The next thing you know, you're on the ground next to the ball and Coach Oliver is running over to you. They get you ice to put on it, but he says you're going to need an X-ray; he thinks your wrist is probably broken.

"That's a real bummer, number 7," the Boys' National Team scout says. You're in too much pain to respond. Your arm is throbbing; your face feels hot with pain and frustration. You're sweating and panting, barely holding it together. "Listen," he continues, "I didn't get to see very much today, but your old coach from Weston speaks very highly of you. Here's my card. Give me a call." You just nod. The pain is so much that you can't even enjoy this moment of possibility.

Go on to the next page.

It feels like everything is a mess. Autumn is angry, your wrist is probably broken, and now you'll be out of play for who knows how long. You wish you could hit the reset button – make different choices. This isn't how it was supposed to turn out.

THE END

Chuck's had quite a few beers, but he seems normal. Maybe just a little louder than usual. You know drinking and driving is stupid, but he must know when he's had too much. He's a senior, after all. You ask him to take you to Bowie's house.

You all pile into Chuck's car. The guys are all yelling and messing around. At first it seems fun, but then Chuck starts paying less attention to the road. No, this is definitely not fun. Unlike them, you're not feeling anything from the beer – you drank one beer over the course of an hour, in little sips, so they wouldn't offer you another – and now you're stuck.

Suddenly, the car starts to veer off into the other lane. You're sitting in the back, but you spring forward, grab the wheel, and yank it to the right before the car goes into oncoming traffic. You hear the sound of a horn blaring. You feel your body tossed to the right. Now you're upside down. There's screaming.

The car has rolled off the road into a ditch. When it stops, almost everyone is silent. You're all in shock. Just one person is still screaming. Davis. He must have had his hand out the window. It looks like hamburger meat and there's blood everywhere. You look frantically for a way to get out. You feel like you're going to be sick.

"Oh man," Chuck yells. "Look at Davis' hand. That's so messed up. Oh man, what are we gonna do?"

"We gotta get out of this car," you hear Darby say, and somehow you all stumble out.

Go on to the next page.

A man is walking toward you from the road. He's asking if everyone is alright. Davis is still howling, and you don't know about anyone else, because you're too busy throwing up.

Needless to say, you do *not* make it to Bowie's birthday dinner. Instead, you spend the night being reprimanded by police, your coach, and your parents. Everyone keeps saying the same thing to all of you: *Why would you make that choice?* You honestly don't know.

Coach Oliver suspends all of you for drinking, and you can't believe your high school soccer career has been put on hold as quickly as it began.

The next day, you call Coach Duncan. He listens silently as you recall the whole horrible event. There's disappointment and concern in his voice, but he offers to let you train with Weston, so that you don't lose your edge.

"Every choice you make has consequences," he says. "Each one leads to a certain outcome. There are no guarantees, and we can't predict the future, but what we can do is listen to our instincts. You've got a compass inside you, Kev, and it'll point you in the right direction, but you choose whether to follow it or try to do things your own way."

You feel like your compass may be broken, but you're determined to get back on track.

THE END

There's no way you're getting in a car with someone who's been drinking. Chuck seems okay, but he's definitely drunk. And you've seen enough of those terrifying ads on TV to scare you away from ever mixing alcohol and driving.

"Thanks anyway, but my sister's on her way to get me," you lie.

You've been at the field for about 45 minutes, and it will probably take you about 15 or 20 minutes to get to Bowie's house. You take off at a jog, hoping to get there before they cut the cake.

Dinner is over, but you're not surprised by that. They were waiting to cut the cake though, so you apologize to everyone, especially Bowie.

You and Bowie sit on the couch with your cake.

"Hey, man, I love that toolbox you made me," he says. Luckily, Sam remembered to drop it off.

"Yeah," you say, excited. "I built it with my grandparents. I'm so glad you like it. Now you won't have to search for years when you need a tool."

"Totally," he agrees. "Did you carve the handle? It's awesome."

You did, and you're proud to admit it. You spent a lot of time making Bowie's toolbox. He *is* one of your best friends after all.

"Hey, where were you anyway?" he asks.

"Some of the seniors asked me to celebrate the win with them. I didn't think we'd be so long though. I'm really sorry, Bowie man."

"It's okay, but were you drinking beer?" he asks, leaning in closer

Go on to the next page.

to your face.

"Uh, kinda," you say, backing away. "I had one."

"Why would you do that?" he asks, sounding annoyed. "That's really not smart."

After a few minutes of silence, Bowie gets up from the couch and goes to sit by Autumn. She's still not speaking to you either. This is perfect. Now both your best friends are mad at you.

You sit there, slowly eating your cake and wondering how you made such a mess of things, and trying to figure out how you can fix it.

What seems like a million years later, since all you've been doing is talking with Bowie's mom and twiddling your thumbs, your mom comes to pick you up. She doesn't look like herself though. Something's wrong. She's not smiling. Also, she kind of rushes you out of the house, which is not like her at all, though right now, you're not complaining. Once you're outside, she grabs you by the shoulders.

"Kevin," she says in an unnaturally serious voice. "Honey, I have to tell you something, but I'm right here for you, okay?"

"Mom, you're kind of freaking me out," you say. She doesn't let go.

"Sweetie," she continues, "there's been an accident."

"What kind of accident?" You're really freaking out now.

"It was a group of older boys from the soccer team," she says.

Go on to the next page.

As what she's saying sinks in, you feel like your legs might give out from under you.

"Kevin, are you okay?" she asks, as you realize she's not just holding onto you anymore, but holding you up. You nod and try to steady yourself.

She tells you they were drinking, which of course you already knew. She tells you they swerved into oncoming traffic, and lastly, she tells you one of them is in critical condition. She doesn't know which boy it is, but she knows they were all hurt badly.

Every time you start to think about how you could have been in that car, your legs wobble beneath you. What would have happened if you'd gone with them? *You* might be the one in critical condition . . or worse.

Your mind flickers to Bowie and Autumn. You realize how lucky you are – if you'd been in that car . . . Well, you'd much rather have them mad at you than never see them again. You may have really screwed up in some ways, and your friendships may be a mess right now, but at least you can still change how things turn out.

THE END

It's confusing enough having feelings for your best friend, but now you have to be jealous too? This is so completely unfair. Chuck Grady is a senior for crying out loud. How are you supposed to compete with that? If she likes him, you don't stand a chance. *But what if you can get him to stop liking *her?

It would be great if you could just walk up to him and say, "Hey, Chuck, how 'bout you back off my girl?" But then you might get your face punched. No, you need a way to ensure he won't be interested in her anymore.

The next day in school, you see Chuck in the hall between classes and go up to him.

"Hey, Chuck," you say, somewhat nervously. "Uh, listen, man." You try to sound more confident. "There's something I've gotta tell you."

"Okay, kid," he says. "I'm listening. What's up?"

"Well, you know that girl you were talking with after practice yesterday?"

"Sure," he says. "Autumn – she's a cutie."

"Yeah, her," you say. "Well, there's something you should know about her before you go thinking she'd be a good prom date or whatever."

"What's that?" he wants to know.

"Well," you say, considering your words very carefully, "you see, she's kind of a weirdo. She doesn't really have any friends. I mean

Go on to the next page.

I only hang out with her because I feel sorry for her. And I've even seen her pick her nose," you add for good measure. Now he will definitely not want to be with her.

As far as you can tell, it's worked, because he scrunches his face up and says, "*Ewww!*" Then he shakes his head and walks away. You feel pretty proud of your plan, certain that Chuck will leave Autumn alone, giving you time to figure out how to tell her that you like her. Maybe you should tell Bowie first and get his reaction. You'll see how you feel when you meet them for lunch.

"What is wrong with you?!" Autumn yells in your face as soon as you walk up to her.

"What?" you say, completely confused.

"What would make you say those things about me?" she asks, tears growing in her eyes. "I thought you were my best friend."

"I . . . " you start, but have no idea what to say.

"Did you think Chuck would think you were cool?" she asks. "Because he doesn't. He's actually a nice guy, but you're a jerk!"

Autumn storms off, leaving you there to wonder exactly what went wrong with your plan. Clearly, Chuck told her what you said. You thought he would leave her alone, but you were wrong. The whole thing has backfired. She hates you, and now Chuck thinks you're an idiot. You may end up getting your face punched after all. This is just great.

You spend the rest of the day avoiding Autumn and feeling

Go on to the next page.

horrible. You can't believe how badly your plan failed and how wrecked things are with her. You have no hope of a girlfriend, and you're not sure you even have a friend anymore. You're also not sure what you'll find at practice, but luckily, Chuck doesn't even say thing. At one point, he catches your eye and just shakes his head disapprovingly at you, but that's all you get. At least he doesn't beat you up.

Right after practice, a junior named Evan comes up and pulls you aside. He's been really kind to you. So far, he's one of the only people who hasn't called you "kid" the whole time.

"I've got a question for you, Faklaw," he says. "I've seen how well you control the ball. It seems like you can move it anywhere you want, and I was wondering if you could help me with that. Only thing is," he continues, "it would need to be on the down-low, because I don't want the guys to know that I'm taking lessons from a freshman."

You're definitely flattered that an upperclassman would ask for your help, but you're not sure what to do.

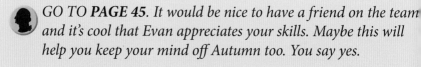

GO TO **PAGE 45**. *It would be nice to have a friend on the team and it's cool that Evan appreciates your skills. Maybe this will help you keep your mind off Autumn too. You say yes.*

GO TO **PAGE 30**. *You're glad that Evan appreciates your skills, but you need to focus on your own game. You apologize and say no.*